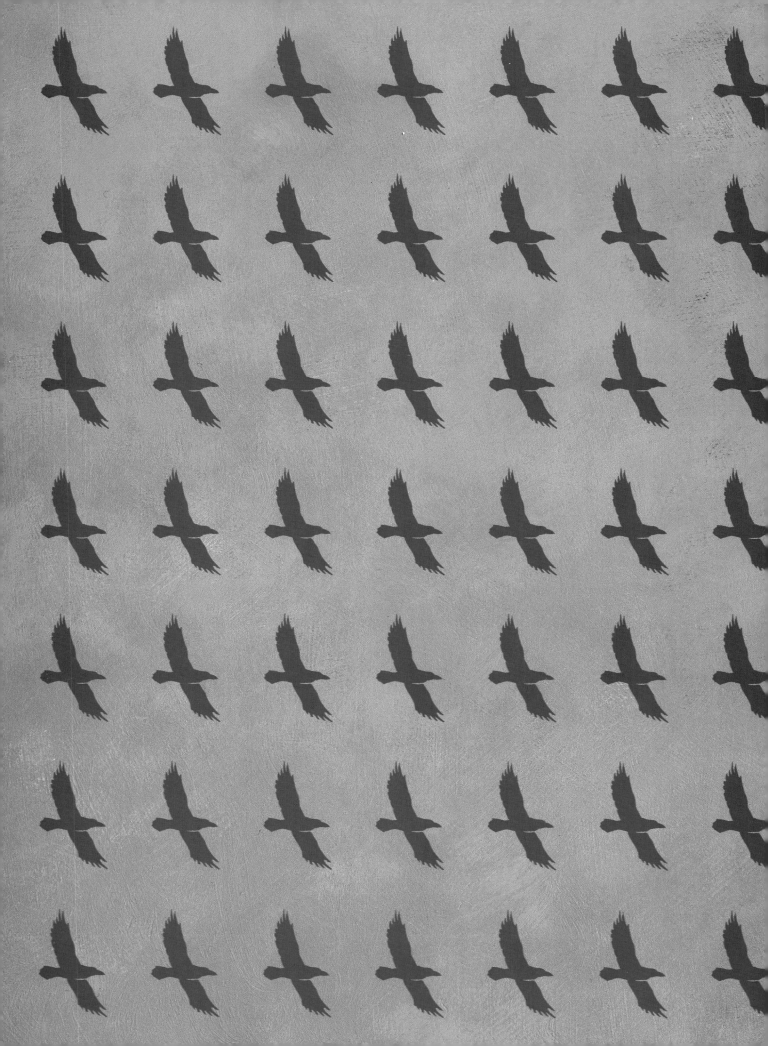

For Franziska

Copyright © 1995 by Nord-Süd Verlag AG, Gossau Zürich, Switzerland
First published in Switzerland under the title *Die 7 Raben*
English translation copyright © 1995 by North-South Books Inc.

All rights reserved.
No part of this book may be reproduced or utilized in any form
or by any means, electronic or mechanical, including photocopying,
recording, or any information storage and retrieval system,
without permission in writing from the publisher.

First published in the United States, Great Britain, Canada,
Australia, and New Zealand in 1995 by North-South Books,
an imprint of Nord-Süd Verlag AG, Gossau Zürich, Switzerland.

Distributed in the United States by North-South Books Inc., New York.

Library of Congress Cataloging-in-Publication Data is available.
A CIP catalogue record for this book is available from The British Library.
ISBN 1-55858-458-7 (TRADE BINDING)
1 3 5 7 9 TB 10 8 6 4 2
ISBN 1-55858-459-5 (LIBRARY BINDING)
1 3 5 7 9 LB 10 8 6 4 2
Printed in Belgium

THE SEVEN RAVENS

A FAIRY TALE BY THE

BROTHERS GRIMM

ILLUSTRATED BY

HENRIETTE SAUVANT

TRANSLATED BY

ANTHEA BELL

NORTH-SOUTH BOOKS

NEW YORK / LONDON

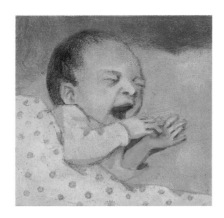

ONCE UPON A TIME there was a man who had seven sons, but he longed for a daughter. One day his wife told him they were going to have another child, and when the baby was born, it was a little girl at last. They were overjoyed, but the baby was small and delicate, so frail that she had to be baptized at once. Her father sent one of the boys hurrying off to the well to fetch water for the baptism. The other six went along with him, and as they jostled one another, each trying to be the first to draw water, they dropped the pitcher into the well. They didn't know what to do, for none of them dared go home.

When they failed to return, their father grew impatient and said, "No doubt those naughty boys have begun playing some game and forgotten." Fearing the little girl would die unbaptized, he cried out in a rage, "I wish the boys were all turned into ravens." No sooner had he said those words than he heard a whirring in the air overhead, and when he looked up, he saw seven ravens black as coal flying away.

The parents could not undo the spell, and they were saddened to have lost their seven sons. But they found some comfort in their dear little daughter, who grew stronger and more beautiful every day. It was a long time before she even knew she had once had brothers, since her parents were careful not to mention them. One day she overheard some people saying that although she was a lovely little girl, she was really to blame for her seven brothers' misfortune. That made her curious, so she went to her mother and father and asked if she had ever had brothers, and where they were now.

Her parents could keep the secret no longer, but they said the spell cast on the boys was heaven's will, and her birth had been only the innocent cause. However, the girl felt it weighing on her mind every day, and she could not rest until she decided to break the spell on her brothers. So she set off into the world in search of them, determined to set them free at any cost. She took nothing with her but a little ring to remind her of her parents, a loaf of bread to satisfy her hunger, a little pitcher of water to quench her thirst, and a little chair to sit on when she felt tired.

She journeyed on and on, far away to the world's end. There she met the sun, but the sun was hot and terrible and ate little children.

She hurried away and went to see the moon, but the moon was cold and cruel and wicked, and on seeing her cried out, "I smell the flesh of a human child."

So she hurried away again and went to see the stars, who were friendly and kind to her. They were all sitting on their own chairs, but the morning star rose, gave the girl the bone of a chicken's leg, and said, "You will find your brothers inside the glass mountain, but you won't be able to get in without this bone."

The girl took the chicken bone, wrapped it in a cloth, and went on again, on and on until she came to the glass mountain. The door was locked, and when she undid the cloth to take out the chicken bone, it was empty. She had lost the gift the kind stars had given her. What could she do now? How could she rescue her brothers without a key to the glass mountain? So the good little sister took a knife, cut off one of her little fingers, put it in the key-hole, and unlocked the door.

Inside the mountain a little dwarf met her. "What are you looking for, my child?" he asked.

"I'm looking for my brothers, the seven ravens," she said.

The dwarf told her, "My masters the ravens are not at home, but if you would like to wait until they return, come in." With these words, he carried in seven plates and seven little cups. The girl ate a morsel of food from each plate and drank a sip from each cup, and into the last cup she dropped the ring she had brought.

Suddenly she heard a whirring and a flapping in the air, and the dwarf said, "Here come my masters flying home."

In they came, hungry and thirsty, and they flew to their plates and cups. "Who's been eating from my plate?" said one raven after another. "Who's been drinking from my cup? A human mouth was here." And when the seventh reached the bottom of his cup, the little ring rolled out. He immediately recognized his parents' ring, and said, "God grant that this ring was brought to us by our sister! For only her presence here will break the spell."

The girl had been hiding behind the door, listening. When she heard his wish, she stepped forward, and all the ravens were turned back into boys again.

So they hugged and kissed each other,
and they all went happily home.

j398.2   Grimm
~~SI~~   ~~Sieben Raben.~~
GR   ~~English.~~

        The seven ravens.

        JUN   1996

DATE			